to Salomé

THIS IS A BORZOI BOOK PUBLISHED BY ALFRED A. KNOPF
Copyright © 1999, 2002 by Hachette Livre
All rights reserved under International and Pan-American
Copyright Conventions. Published in the United States of
America by Alfred A. Knopf, a division of Random House, Inc.,
New York, and simultaneously in Canada by Random House of
Canada Limited, Toronto. Distributed by Random House, Inc.,
New York. Originally published in France as Le cadeau de Noël
by Hachette Jeunesse in 1999. KNOPF, BORZOI BOOKS, and the
colophon are registered trademarks of Random House, Inc.
www.randomhouse.com/kids Library of Congress Cataloging-in-
Publication data Gutman, Anne. Gaspard and Lisa's Christmas
Surprise / Anne Gutman, Georg Hallensleben. p. cm.
Summary: Gaspard and Lisa run into problems when they make
a Christmas gift for their teacher. ISBN 0-375-82229-1
[1. Christmas—Fiction. 2. Gifts—Fiction.] I. Hallensleben, Georg.
II. Title. PZ7.G9844   Gao 2002 [E]—dc21   2001038842
First Borzoi Books edition: September 2002
Printed in France   10 9 8 7 6 5 4 3 2 1

Gaspard and Lisa's Christmas Surprise

Alfred A. Knopf ❧ New York

It was almost Christmas, and Gaspard
and I still hadn't found a present
for our teacher, Mrs. Dupont.

"Lisa, what do you say we give her my old water pistol or my skates from last Christmas?" said Gaspard.

But I said no.
None of our
ideas seemed
right for
Mrs. Dupont.

Then I remembered something.

Mrs. Dupont rides to school on her bike, and when it rains she gets wet. We could make her a raincoat. We had everything in Gaspard's house that we needed to make it.

We put a chair in the bathtub . . .

. . . and I gave the shower curtain a big yank. Down it came.

Then Gaspard posed as my model. He stood on
a kitchen stool to be as tall as Mrs. Dupont.
I wrapped the shower curtain around him. We
couldn't find any needles and thread to sew it
together, so I glued it together with Krazy Glue.
"I'm done," I said to Gaspard. "You can take
it off now."

But he couldn't.

I pushed and I pulled, but he was glued tight inside. Luckily, I had a good idea. . . .

"I'll just cut the curtain," I told Gaspard.

But there was one problem. If Gaspard's parents saw Mrs. Dupont's raincoat, they would recognize it as their missing shower curtain.

"We'll dye it a different color in the washing machine!" said Gaspard.

We put the raincoat in the machine and dumped in some yellow dye.

When the machine stopped,
we took out the raincoat.
"OH, NO!" we both shouted.
The raincoat was still red, and it had
shrunk so much that even Gaspard
couldn't fit into it. Now we had
nothing to give Mrs. Dupont
for Christmas.

Then my best idea yet came to me. The raincoat was too small for Mrs. Dupont, but if we cut two holes in the hood, it would be just right for Pierre.

Mrs. Dupont was very pleased with our present. I bet she thought it was the best present of them all . . .

. . . and I'm sure Pierre did!